LOVE BECOME SERVICE

THE INTEGRATION OF THE SACRAMENTS OF MATRIMONY AND HOLY ORDERS IN THE MINISTRY AND LIFE OF THE MARRIED PERMANENT DEACON

LOVE BECOME SERVICE

THE INTEGRATION OF THE SACRAMENTS OF MATRIMONY AND HOLY ORDERS IN THE MINISTRY AND LIFE OF THE MARRIED PERMANENT DEACON

REV. MSGR. Michael J. Chaback, KCSH, STD

DUFOUR EDITIONS INC.

First published in the United States of America, 2013
by Dufour Editions Inc., Chester Springs, Pennsylvania 19425

ISBN 978-0-8023-1357-7

Cover Image ©Inthename-Stock: inthename-stock.deviantart.com

Nihil Obstat: Rev. Msgr. James J. Mulligan, S.T.L.
Censor Librorum
Imprimatur: Most Rev. John O. Barres, D.D.
Bishop of Allentown
The Nihil Obstat and Imprimatur are a declaration that a book or pamphlet is considered to be free from doctrinal or moral error. It is not implied that those who have granted the Nihil Obstat and Imprimatur agree with the contents, opinions or statements expressed.

Library of Congress Cataloging-in-Publication Data

Chaback, Michael J., 1943-
  Love become service : the integration of the sacraments of matrimony and holy orders in the ministry and life of the married permanent deacon / Rev. Msgr. Michael J. Chaback, KCSH, STD.
    pages cm
  Includes bibliographical references and index.
  ISBN-13: 978-0-8023-1357-7 (pbk.)
  ISBN-10: 0-8023-1357-4 (pbk.)
  1. Deacons--Catholic Church. I. Title.
  BX1912.C425 2013
  253'.22088282--dc23

                                        2013033827

Printed and bound in the United States of America

A theological essay based upon number sixty-one of the
<u>*Directory For The Ministry And Life Of Permanent Deacons*</u>,
promulgated by the Congregation of the Clergy
on 22 February 1998.

CONTENTS

To the deacons of the Diocese of Allentown and their wives,
so many of whom have assisted me in my ministry and
shared with me the bonds both of discipleship and friendship.

**"By the standards of this world servanthood
is despised, but in the wisdom and providence
of God it is the mystery through which Christ
redeems the world. And you are ministers
of that mystery, heralds of that Gospel."**

–Blessed John Paul II, Address to the
Permanent Deacons of the United States
Detroit: 19 September 1987

INTRODUCTION

The following reflection was written as a pastoral response
to a concern shared by many of the wives of our permanent deacons and to address a lacuna in my own understanding. Most diaconal couples readily recognize that it is
the husband who is ordained and not the wife. The wife's
role is commonly expressed as making her husband's
becoming a deacon possible by her willingly giving affirmation and support. Many certainly have done so and
have experienced a positive and spiritually enriching journey together with their husbands. But there are also some
whose experience has been less than positive and who,
more often than not, remain silent.

At a roundtable with some of our diaconal wives, even
those who consistently support their husbands in their ministry lamented the loss of the joy of worshiping at Mass
together as a couple, and of the nourishment given their
marriage by doing so. What they shared in that conversation has continued to echo in my mind. Prior to that
moment, I had already begun to seek a clearer understanding of the ideal role the deacon's marriage ought to play in
his diaconal identity and ministry. Incidental statements in

a variety of Church documents suggested that more was to be asserted here than I had previously acknowledged. I began to intuit that somehow a dynamism of mutual enrichment was occurring between the two sacramental realities that a married ordained deacon was living. Understanding it and giving it expression became a recurrent concern in my thoughts.

I have undertaken this reflection then, not only out of my own intellectual need, but more so as a possible contribution to the ongoing enrichment of our present diaconal couples and also to the authentic formation of our diaconal candidates and their wives. While far from complete, I offer these thoughts as a hopefully legitimate and substantive beginning of a much needed and deeper appreciation of the interplay of the two sacraments that rightfully claim the heart of the married permanent deacon.

The essay formed the basis of the summer component of our diaconal formation program in 2012, which was an at-home five-week structured interaction between our married candidates and their wives. Each Monday they received a section of the text with reflection questions added to guide their conversation. By all accounts the process fulfilled a deeply felt need and proved very helpful to their spiritual growth. The reflection questions are provided here as well, but have been modified to facilitate their use by deacons and their wives.

61.a "The Sacrament of Matrimony sanctifies conjugal love and constitutes it a sign of the love with which Christ gives himself to the Church (cf. Ephesians 5:25). It is a gift from God and should be a source of nourishment for the spiritual life of those deacons who are married. Since family life and professional responsibilities must necessarily reduce the amount of time which married deacons can dedicate to the ministry, it will be necessary to integrate these various elements in a unitary fashion, especially by means of shared prayer. In marriage, love becomes an interpersonal giving of self, a mutual fidelity, a source of new life, a support in times of joy and sorrow: in short, love becomes service. When lived in faith, this *family service* is for the rest of the faithful an example of the love of Christ. The married deacon must use it as a stimulus of his diakonia in the Church".

For the Christian believer, whose life has been inserted by the Sacrament of Baptism into the mystery of the divine self-communication in Christ, the love attraction that is experienced and expressed in the intimacy of married life is so elevated by that baptismal solidarity as to become a true participation in the divine love itself. The love between a husband and wife is no longer a mere natural reality but becomes an effective sign of the love that is God and that the Father bestows upon us in Jesus Christ. Inserted into the Mystery of the Church, the baptized married couple concretely images within the community of the redeemed its own identity as the Bride of Christ.

- *What does being baptized mean to you? As a man? As a woman?*

- *What does being baptized mean to you as a couple?*

- *Would your married life be any different if you had never been baptized and had been married in a merely civil ceremony? Explain your answer.*

Within this mystery then, Christian married love is an illustrative gift, a grace that transforms two limited human beings into witnesses to the same powers that characterize the divine love itself. As God's love for us is faithful, permanent, and life-giving, so now are Christian spouses able to love one another in the same manner, a manner that far exceeds the innate powers of their human nature. Arising from the personal love of the Father and the Son, which is the Holy Spirit, Christian married love, as an encounter with God, further calls these same two divinely empowered individuals to their own personal response to the Source of their new life. They express that response in a gracious and sincere commitment to live in conscious fidelity to what they have now become, for their own fulfillment and for the sake of the Church.

• *Do you believe that your love for each other is different in any way because you were married as Christians?*

• *How have you understood your marriage vows? Why does the Church hold them to be binding on Christian marriage?*

• *Do you attribute your growth as a married couple in any way to the grace and power of the Sacrament of Matrimony? Explain your answer.*

As a gift of God, their sacramental reality cannot be separated out from the person of the husband who becomes a deacon of the Church. By the grace of one and the same God and the laying on of hands, he is now conformed to Christ the Servant. He becomes a living sign of that servanthood for the sake of the Body of Christ, the Church. As a person who has now been transformed into a living sign of both the nature of the divine love, revealed in its faithful, permanent and life-giving dynamisms, and the servant-form it assumes in its concrete communication to human life in Jesus Christ, the married permanent deacon faces the deeply personal exigency of integrating into one life both the Sacrament of Matrimony and the Sacrament of Holy Orders. This integration is the hinge of his personal fulfillment as a husband and as a deacon. These two gifts received from the one God must harmonize and unite in the one person who has received them.

• *How have you experienced the challenge of harmonizing your life as husband and wife with the demands of the diaconate?*

• *How successful have you been so far? What difficulties have you encountered and how have you dealt with them?*

Viewed from this perspective, the oft-quoted priority paradigm of God, wife, family, work, and ministry actually projects a misleading image of the task facing the married deacon. Prioritizing the elements of his life, however necessary that might be in terms of concerns and responsibilities, may effectively contribute nothing to the unity that should be achieved. Prioritizing all too readily compartmentalizes life rather than integrates it. The married deacon is certainly responsible to remain faithful to all the obligations of his personal religious life, of his marital state, of his family life, of the work by which he supports his family, and of his diaconal ministry in the Church. Time constraints alone, however, testify to the frustrating futility of his giving due attention to all that lies within his care, if his varied obligations are viewed separately. They will inevitably compete with one another for his humanly limited time and energy. He will make choices which, being necessary and unavoidable,will divide his heart, and most likely be misunderstood by others. The integration of his life becomes a necessity not only for his own well-being, but also for those whose lives he touches and to whom he has committed himself. His attention to one responsibility will in all probability be perceived by some of them, and possibly also by himself,as a lack of commitment, or even an infidelity, to another.

• *Have you tried prioritizing your present obligations to marriage and to diaconal ministry? Has it always worked? If not, why not? How do you deal with it when it doesn't work?*

• *Have you ever felt that you were somehow failing in one responsibility by giving time and energy to another? Have you ever felt misunderstood because of this?*

• *Has this ever become a source of tension in your marriage?*

• *Has it ever become a source of tension for you in your present diaconal assignment?*

Consider this scenario. Deacon Tom is assigned to a parish where he is required to assist with communion at all Sunday Masses, in addition to the one at which he actually serves at the altar. In practice, as an ordained man, he is expected to be as available on weekends as are the priests assigned to the parish. He is presently under great stress at work, where overtime has become all too common because of corporate downsizing. His father has just passed away and, as executor, he is responsible for settling the estate. When he requests to be excused for several weekends because of the burdens of this task, his pastor reacts negatively. He actually accuses him of not living up to his vocation as a deacon. He further comments that such behavior suggests that he might not really even have a ministerial vocation. The other priests in their own way echo the remark.

• *Imagine yourself in Tom's situation. What would your feelings be towards your pastor? Towards the other priests in the parish?*

What's happening here? Having to make choices in a very stressful situation, Deacon Tom is further burdened by the reaction of the priests of the parish who perceive his decision-making as flawed and as a withdrawal from his responsibilities to the Church. Is it possible that the priests, as celibate ordained men, are instinctively viewing the deacon's situation from a personal perspective that has never had the challenge of integrating two sacramental realities? Are they then, with all good intentions, treating the married deacon as though he were a full-time celibate minister and in their expectations of him becoming critical when he is constrained by a pressing family concern? In their mind then, ministry responsibilities must be honored above all else. As he turns his attention to his family, his diminished ability to fulfill his diaconal ministry is perceived as a lack of commitment, as an infidelity.

- *Do you think there's any reality to this scenario?*

- *Do you think that some priests might prioritize responsibilities very differently than you do as married?*

Consider now another scenario. Deacon Miguel has really taken to his new role in the Church as a deacon. He enjoys being at the altar for Mass on Saturday evening and again on Sunday morning. He regularly preaches at least once every weekend. He supervises the Saint Vincent DePaul Society, participates in the RCIA program, and shares the many home Communion visits with the pastor. While he enjoys preaching, he finds preparing a homily challenging and spends an hour or so several nights a week working on it. His wife is beginning to resent the fact that they no longer have the same quality time together as they once had. From the time he first joined the formation program she has been anxious that his diaconate might jeopardize their retirement plans. Was she now to lose the dreams she had for the later years of their life? Maybe this is not going to work out at all. She's beginning to wonder whether he now loves the diaconate more than he loves her. As he gives more of himself and of his time to his ministry, his diminished ability to be present to her and to her needs is felt as a hurtful loss, as an infidelity.

• *How real do you think this scenario could be?*

• *How might a deacon's wife come to feel that her husband's ministry is depriving their life together of some things that should be rightfully be theirs?*

Adding new responsibilities to ones we already have often merely lengthens the list of what must be done. Given our limited humanity, can the list eventually get too long for everything to be done well, if at all? With this approach, do we not in practice then take care of some things and shortchange others? We might muddle through if we were merely dealing with material tasks. Can such an approach, however, really work if what we need to do ultimately affects other persons and their lives? The married deacon who merely prioritizes his commitments by following a fixed paradigm, and does not integrate them, will eventually suffer for it and alienate some, at the very least, of the persons to whom he once promised himself.

Demonstrating the pitfalls of prioritizing and the corresponding need for integration is relatively easy. Life itself makes the case. But having done that, the challenge of actually determining how to achieve the necessary integration becomes not only an abstract psychological problem and, in our case, a theological one as well, but also a deeply felt personal need. For the person actually living the reality, the only alternative to an authentic integration is the enduring and debilitating heartache of a divided life.

- *Can merely prioritizing our responsibilities by itself ever be a real solution to our need to unify the varied elements of our lives?*

- *What is the weakness in a prioritizing approach?*

- *What price will you pay if you do not find a satisfactory solution to unify your life as a married man and a deacon in the Church?*

- *How will a failure here affect your wife and family? How will it affect the people you serve in your ministry?*

This issue is not without parallel in ministerial spirituality. While not facing the challenge of integrating two life sacraments, priests still experience their own unique personal need to integrate the various dimensions of their commitments and responsibilities. Again, within human limitations, how does one person faithfully fulfill the demands of his personal religiosity, of his family bonds, of his own intellectual and social needs, of an authentic celibate life, and of his sacramental identity and pastoral commitments? Theological reflection on the priesthood has fortunately matured to the point where it is a genuinely received teaching that this integration is achieved in and through a spirituality centered on pastoral charity, *caritas pastoralis*, or, as I like to put it, shepherd love.

The priest who roots his personal identity in the love exemplified by the Model Shepherd in the Gospel of John will be enabled to live consistently the harmony and balance that gathers into one all the dimensions of his life. Whatever a good shepherd is about, he knows that laying down his life in solidarity with all who are loved by God is the governing principle that identifies him and establishes his interior peace and ministerial authenticity. Pastoral charity is the hinge pin that enables the priest to hold together in harmony all that matters in his life and all that has been entrusted to him. It guides and animates all his decisions so that he leads with true integrity one life communicating the one holiness of God and the one love of Jesus Christ. Living his daily life in the abiding consciousness of his personal consecration to witness the self-gift of the Eternal Son, the priest remains faithful to his identity and responsibilities, and personally is at peace with himself, in all that he does. He now can respond to the exigencies of his life, not by recourse to a fixed hierarchy of responsibilities, but by a decision process governed by the qualities of the Model Shepherd. Pastoral charity integrates his life.

- *What is the difference between prioritizing responsibilities and what ideally can and should happen in the life of a priest?*

- *What do you see as the key elements in this particular model for integrating life?*

- *Think of a priest that you know whose life appears to be held together by his imitation of the Good Shepherd. Can you see in his life how "pastoral charity" is the hinge pin that unifies his many responsibilities?*

- *If you know such a priest, talk with him about his experience of "holding it all together."*

Contemplating the spiritual integration of the priest, might we not affirm a similar integrating principle, a similar hinge-pin, in the life of a married permanent deacon? It may indeed be as near as the principle that emerges from Christian marriage's transformation of human love into divine love, the principle of love-become-service, *amor servitium factus*. The natural love of the spouses, one for the other, in its sacramental dialogue with the love of God is transformed into the kind of love proclaimed by Saint Paul in his first letter to the Corinthians. It becomes a love patient and kind, bearing all things, believing all things, hoping all things, and enduring all things. It is a love that delights only in the achieved good of the beloved.

- *Has your love for each other evolved over the years of your marriage? How so?*

- *Have you experienced "love-become-service" in your life together? Share some examples of when you touched with each other the kind of love of which Saint Paul speaks.*

- *How important is this kind of love in a Christian marriage?*

- *What might such love someday ask of a partner in a marriage?*

Such is the love of the Trinity as it has been revealed to us in the economy of salvation. Imaging the love of the Father, the Son and the Holy Spirit, Christian married love reveals to the spouses the transcendent depth of their own personhood through the self-gift, one to the other, now made possible by the grace of God. Through their mutual and lasting fidelity they discover themselves and the deepest meaning of our common humanity. In the purity and totality of their self-gift they become one with God in bringing forth a new life into the world. Holding fast to the divine love that is now their love, they are one in both joy and sorrow. In the power of this love they serve one another, enabling each one's truest self-discovery and ultimate creativity. Love has fulfilled itself in becoming service.

• *How has your love for each another contributed to your own sense of your personal identity and worth?*

• *How has your love for each other enabled you to become good parents?*

For the two united in Christian marriage love-become-service is not only the fulfillment of their human attraction and desire, but is in effect the integrating principle, the hinge pin, that enables the harmony and unity of all their decision-making, whether together as a couple in the indissoluble unity of their one flesh or distinctly as individuals in the incommunicable depths of their own hearts. Whether in their responsibilities to their children or in their obligations to their extended families and the human community, at work or at play, decisions shaped by love-become-service will never divide their hearts nor betray their union.

Essential to the living of the new sacramental reality of the Christian married couple is the bringing to their abiding consciousness this dynamism of grace by which God is transforming their love and empowering their lives. Through awareness of their love becoming service they can bring an informed deliberateness to their decision-making, and so actively harmonize the many and varied aspects of their daily lives. Obviously the fostering of such decision-making requires mutual presence, reflection and acceptance of the love-become-service principle. As baptized and believing spouses, the tool for growth that they must employ with regularity is shared prayer.

- *How do you ordinarily make decisions as a married couple?*

- *How do you ordinarily make your individual decisions?*

- *How do you ensure that your mutual decisions and your individual ones are never at odds with each other?*

- *What would be the impact on your lives if both your mutual and individual decisions were consciously and deliberately made in fidelity to "love-become-service?"*

- *What do you have to do to make this happen habitually?*

All genuine prayer opens us to God's perspective on our lives and disposes us to the power of divine grace. The Christian spouses who reflect together in the invoked presence of God are best situated to orient rightly their marriage and their lives. Encountering one another and each other's needs in prayer is a genuine expression of their love becoming service. At the same time, it enables them to grasp more readily the implications of that dynamism for the strengthening of their bond and their persons, and for the governing of their decision-making. Shared prayer then becomes an effective tool for bringing into habitual consciousness the hinge pin that will make them of one mind and one heart in all they do.

- *What is your experience of sharing prayer together as a married couple?*

- *If you do pray together, how do you ensure that your prayer is the prayer of a couple living one life rather than the prayer of two individuals merely praying in the same place at the same time?*

- *What do you pray about?*

- *If you do not pray together regularly, what prevents you from doing so?*

Love-become-service, which in this context the *Directory* also calls family service, is the practical form the divine love assumes in sacramental union with the Christian married couple. It is the visible shape of their witness before the Church of the love of Jesus Christ. It is then what the married man brings as an essential part of his personhood to his service of Christ in the permanent diaconate. Love-become-service as the fruit of his marriage becomes the stuff at the heart of his self-gift to a fruitful diaconal ministry. In his sacramental dialog with Christ the Servant what he brings from his marriage will be transformed by divine grace, like the clay in the hands of the potter, into a broader love-become-service that will build up and unify the People of God. It is now evident in a more profound way why it is that the Church invites to the diaconate men who already are known for their service to their parish and local community.

involvement in her husband's public ministry. This is so much more than her merely making it possible for him to be a deacon by her affirmation and support. This is much more than a permissive "yes" to his diaconate. Her assent must genuinely include a more explicit and conscious commitment to their continued growth together in the love that characterizes Christian marriage, to mutual sacrificial love, to love-become-service, to the divine love itself. Her assent is a commitment to offer their marriage explicitly to the service of the Church. The wives of deacons then are truly, in the words of the Holy Father, "close collaborators in their ministry, and are likewise challenged with them to grow in the knowledge and love of Jesus Christ."

- *How have you understood to this point the wife's role in her husband's desire to become a deacon?*

- *Reflect together on the understanding of the wife's role being presented here. How comfortable are you with it?*

- *How do you see yourselves as a diaconal couple "offering your marriage to the service of the Church?"*

Now all of this is obviously the ideal, that which a true diaconal marriage ought to be. While it is important to assert that ideal in a clear and uncompromising manner, we would fail in our ministry to the deacon and his wife were we not to recognize the reality of the human condition which is often far from what is desired. Progress in love-becoming-service for most, if not all, married couples is not a simple linear development that knows no difficulties or frustrations, no setbacks or failures. Like the Christian life itself it is defined more by its commitment to a continued striving forward than by the milestones actually achieved. What is important is that the goal, what ought to be, is acknowledged and the means necessary to strive toward it be consistently and deliberately employed. In matters of authentic love the Church has constantly affirmed that there is no more potent and necessary source of strength than the virtue of chastity.

- *How have you handled the difficulties and struggles that you have experienced in your life together as a married couple?*

- *What supports do you believe a husband and wife need to never give up on each other, but rather to continue to strive forward as a Christian married couple?*

Blessed John Paul II, in his *Apostolic Exhortation on the Role of the Christian Family in the Modern World (Familiaris Consortio)* in 1981, characterized chastity in a uniquely positive manner as a "spiritual energy capable of defending love from the perils of selfishness and aggressiveness, and able to advance it toward its full realization." Contrary to many popular depictions of chastity as a rejection of human sexuality and of its role in human development, John Paul saw it as a positive factor in the development of authentic maturity and, as he already had reflected upon at great length in his *Catechesis on the Book of Genesis* during his Wednesday audiences from 1979 through 1980, as fostering the nuptial meaning of the human body. Chastity is a passionate zeal in the pursuit of authentic love and consequently an equally passionate and unyielding resistance to all that corrupts it. Chastity in marriage is the mutual and committed passion of the spouses to advance their journey into love-become-service and to resist any compromise with a lesser goal. Chastity in a diaconal marriage places that passion publicly at the service of the Lord Jesus. Both spouses are personally and intimately involved in the whole of this. At its heart it is meant to become their constant and common labor, and their truest joy.

- *What was your initial reaction to the statement about chastity as a source of strength in Christian marriage? How have you understood chastity to this point?*

- *If "chastity in marriage is the mutual and committed passion of the spouses to advance their journey into love-become-service and to resist any compromise with a lesser goal," is your marriage then a chaste marriage?*

Just as an abiding interior solitude is nurtured and sustained by exterior silence, so can chastity, even in marriage, be supported by continence, willingly embraced from time to time. An occasional shift from the ordinary bodily expression of a married couple's mutual love to a more reserved and focused engagement of their spiritual union can powerfully nourish their commitment to direct the whole of their married experience to its fulfillment in love-become-service. Continence then, like silence, becomes a tool, periodically useful to hone their passion for authentic love, so that every expression of love in their lives is part of their own growth towards its fulfillment. However intimate and personal this is to them, it will eventually manifest itself in the ministry of the married deacon. While a diaconal couple is under no particular obligation in this regard, whatever is useful in moving them forward on their spousal journey, moves also the husband's diaconal service to its proper authenticity, its own witness to love-become-service.

> • *Do you appreciate this recommendation of periodic continence, i.e., sexual self-restraint, especially from sexual intercourse, as a valuable tool in a married couple's pursuit of authentic love? Or is it merely the well-intentioned but misguided advice of myopic celibates?*

> • *Have such moments of self-restraint ever been a positive part of your own marriage experience? If so, how have they helped you? If not, might you now be willing to consider an occasional experiment?*

The deacon, who because of the passionate commitment to authentic love formed in him through a focused Christian marriage brings that same zeal to his ministry, will be empowered to resist successfully all manipulative and self-centered behaviors. The criteria by which he measures the outcomes of his efforts will be those of the gospel of self-giving rather than those of the secular world. Even something as ordinary as the use of his time will ultimately find itself ordered by the love at the core of his life, rather than being spent in ephemeral pursuits of questionable value. Bringing that same zeal to bear on his diaconal ministry, the married deacon will readily recognize that all whom he encounters are to be treasured by him because they are treasured by God. They are to be served by him because they have first been served by Jesus Christ. His marital chastity will not only move him toward an abiding tenderness in the intimacy of his union with his wife, but will so shape within him a gentleness of spirit that will enable him to both encourage and comfort all whose lives he touches. Rooted in authentic love, both in his marriage and in his ministry, he will in the end come to see as God sees. This perspective will illumine his mind and heart with the sentiments of Jesus Christ, "who, though he was in the form of God, did not regard equality with God something to be grasped. Rather, he emptied himself, taking the form of a slave..." (Philippians 2: 6-7)

- *How close are you as a married couple to seeing "the gospel of self-giving" reflected in your married life?*

- *Have you ever experienced your lives as being almost spontaneously ordered by the love you have come to share together? Share some memories of such moments with each other.*

- *Can you see how this carries over into diaconal ministry? Reflect together on how abiding tenderness in marriage becomes gentleness of spirit in ministry?*

- *Do you know diaconal couples in whom you have seen this happen? Consider talking with them about it.*

The wives of deacons then are truly "close collaborators in their ministry." This assertion of Blessed John Paul II is no mere recognition of a wife's necessary permission and cooperation; it is rather the affirmation of a powerful formative dynamism at the very heart of the married deacon's identity and mission. From his wife and together with her, the one man who is both husband and deacon learns how to love in the self-giving manner that fulfills both his marriage and his ordination. As he and his wife evolve into a couple whose union is defined by mutual love-become-service, his ability to witness the servanthood of Christ to the Church is perfected. Their marital union becomes a genuine source of grace for his diaconate.

- *How do you now understand the connection between your pursuing love-become-service in your marriage and the husband becoming/being a truly good deacon?*

- *Reflect together on how your marriage becomes a true source of grace for the diaconate, i.e., on how your marriage "gifts" his ministry?*

- *Is this asking too much of you? Describe your feelings to each other.*

61c. "Special care should be taken to ensure that the families of deacons be made aware of the demands of the diaconal ministry. The spouses of married deacons, who must give their consent to their husband's decision to seek ordination to the diaconate, should be assisted to play their role with joy and discretion. They should esteem all that concerns the Church, especially the duties assigned to their husbands. For this reason it is opportune that they should be kept duly informed of their husbands' activities in order to arrive at a harmonious balance between family, professional and ecclesial responsibilities. In the children of married deacons, where such is possible, an appreciation of their father's ministry can also be fostered. They in turn should be involved in the apostolate and give coherent witness in their lives."

• *How the diaconate changed your life as a married couple and as a family?*

• *Has there been any estrangement in your married relationship or with your children because of it? If yes, how so? How have you addressed it?*

Practically, this means that the Church must act decisively on its responsibility, not only to ensure the human, spiritual, intellectual, and pastoral formation of the deacon, but also to form his wife and children, so that they might remain one with him as he takes on new and current obligations as an ordained man. His wife especially should experience his diaconate with the joy that accompanies the Gospel's proclamation of the unmerited nearness of God revealed in Jesus. However advanced may be her personal spiritual awareness, the Church is obliged to assist her in appreciating how important she is in the design of God, a design that has placed her husband within apostolic ministry. The joy she has known through their mutual growth in love-become-service must now become one with the Church's joy in receiving her husband's gift of himself. For both her and the Church, their joy becomes all the greater as she gives birth with her husband to a new witness of that same love in his diaconal ministry. Through their union in love-become-service, she is not only the wife of a deacon, but becomes in a mystical way the mother of his ministry.

• *Can you, as the wife of a deacon, honestly say that you are "joyful" at what your husband is doing as a deacon? If so, what has helped you? If not, what's the problem and how might it be addressed?*

• *How might the Church do more to help the wives of deacons and deacons themselves appreciate how important they are in the design of God?*

The Church then must help the deacon's wife grasp this vision and learn to treasure it in her heart. However, what she has become does not only lead to joy, it wil also ask of her a certain self-denial. This too the Church must help her to embrace. What her deacon husband gives to the Church could never be given without her, and yet, in the end, it is he who is the deacon, who in ministry alone publicly signs the servanthood of Christ. Like Mary, the Mother of the Redeemer, she will often find herself looking on from afar. As Mary learned, she too must learn when to speak and when to be silent, when to stand beside the one for whom she cares the most, and when to stand aside. She will need to acquire the strength of a prudent spirit and a discerning heart, knowing what is the right thing to do and how to do it at the right time. She will always need to be present to her husband, and the power of her presence can never be discounted. But presence takes many forms, and knowing how to choose among them in the varied moments of his ministry will always be her challenge. Helping her acquire the strength and the wisdom she will need is the responsibility of the Church that called her husband to become a deacon.

• *Have you, as the wife of a deacon, already experienced a measure of aloneness and self-denial because of your husband's commitment to the diaconate? If so, share some examples of it with your husband.*

• *Do you, as a deacon, see and value the presence of your wife at all times in your ministry, even when she is not physically there? If so, share some examples of that with her.*

• *Is there anything the Church can do in to help you in these needs?*

Part of the help the Church needs to give to the wife of a deacon, especially during the years of candidacy, is a deepened knowledge and appreciation of our Catholic faith, above all, of our beliefs regarding Christ and the Church, of Christian marriage and apostolic ministry. While there is much in her husband's formation that is not strictly necessary to her formation as a deacon's wife, the more she understands and esteems the mystery in which she is intimately involved, the more informed is her consent and the more active will be her role in the integration of the two sacraments that are joined in their common life. It is therefore incumbent upon the Church to provide for her human, spiritual, intellectual and pastoral formation in an appropriate way that is distinct from her husband's and particular to her own needs.

• *As the wife of a deacon, do you believe that it is as important for you to deepen your own knowledge and appreciation of our Catholic Faith as it is indeed nesessary for your husband to do so as a deacon? If so, how have you been doing that? If not, why not?*

• *Is there any other way in which we might help you in this?*

Particular concern must be given to ensuring her thorough understanding of the specific role her husband now has in the daily life of the Christian community. She should never be surprised by what his diaconal service in the ministry of the word, of the altar, and of charity might ask of him as a duty and responsibility. From the first days of Aspirancy to her husband's retirement from assigned diaconal ministry, she needs be made aware of all commitments that oblige him, especially those formally made through agreements of service. This is necessary because of the active role that is rightfully hers as a result of the divine mystery that is their Christian marriage, a role that she is meant to fulfill together with him in the integration of their marital union and his diaconal ministry, and indeed of all the elements of both their lives.

• *As the wife of a deacon, are you generally aware of your husband's responsibilities and commitments in his ministry? If not, what might help improve this for you?*

It is important in reflecting on this integration of Christian Marriage and Holy Orders to address the concerns of the children of the married deacon. No matter their age, they are intimately part of a family whose life is significantly altered by the ministerial commitment of its father. They, as well as their mother, need to understand and value their father's diaconal identity and responsibilities. Even a minimal perception of their father's diaconate as threatening to their relationship with him could easily magnify and distort the natural breaking-away that occurs as children pass into adulthood, a breaking-away that could even distance them from their faith. Their father's dedication to the Church cannot without damage be perceived by his children as a personal loss.

• *What's your initial reaction to Blessed John Paul's inclusion of a particular call to witness the divine plan for marriage within the vocation of the married permanent deacon and his wife?*

• *How comfortable are you with this notion of a vocation, not only for the husband, but for the married couple itself, and therefore for the wife as well?*

• *What impact does this have on your life as a diaconal couple?*

This inclusion of the life witness of the married couple within the diaconal mission is clearly a major expansion of what being a deacon means for most people. While not a defining element of the diaconate, it is a genuine existential element of the diaconate of a married man. As such, the married deacon is actually performing diaconal ministry as he and his wife live the day-to-day realities of a married couple, a Christian married couple committed to fulfilling their union in the love-become-service that is not only their vocation, but is also the heart of the self-communication of God in Jesus Christ. What they ordinarily do as a married couple becomes through diaconate ordination a servant ministry to other families, both in the Church and in the world.

• *Can you think of some practical ways in which what you do in the ordinary living of your life as a Christian married couple might become a servant ministry to other families? Spend some time together talking about this.*

• *How might your approach, again as a Christian couple, to parenting and grand-parenting be an important
part of your service witness to other families?*

A particular facet of this ministry is their daily demonstration of the integration of the responsibilities toward
God, marriage, family, work, and service, which integration is necessary for well-being for all married couples,
especially those within the Church. Their struggle for harmony in the whole of their life, done consistently and with
a faith inspired hope, is the gift they are meant to give to
others. The presence of diaconal married couples in the
midst of the Church community is further seen by John
Paul as a service, rendered in the form of encouragement,
to all who are engaged in family life ministries. The diaconal couple then is also meant to serve as a model for
what those who actively promote the good of families seek
to achieve. It is not enough then that a particular Church
community knows that its deacon has a wife and a family
life. The community, in all moments of its life, must see
them together as a couple, as a diaconal married couple
offering to all their witness of love-becoming-service.

• *Do you appreciate how important your married life
has becomes to the Church as a diaconal couple?
Assess together your readiness for this.*

• *Share some examples of the love-become-service that
already is part of your experience as a married couple. Recognize and celebrate the good that already is
yours.*

• *What can you do as a couple over the next year (a year at a time is enough...) to develop and deepen love-become-service in your life? What issues might you expect to encounter that could become opportunities for this? Be specific.*

A Summary of the Main Points of the Commentary

1. Inserted into the Mystery of the Church, the baptized married couple concretely images within the community of the redeemed its own identity as the Bride of Christ.

2. As God's love for us is faithful, permanent, and life-giving, so now are Christian spouses able to love one another in the same manner, a manner that far exceeds the innate powers of their human nature.

3. The married permanent deacon, as a person who has now been transformed into a living sign of both the nature of the divine love, revealed in its faithful, permanent and life-giving dynamisms, and the servant form it assumes in its concrete communication to human life in Jesus Christ, faces the deeply personal exigency of integrating into one life both the Sacrament of Matrimony and the Sacrament of Holy Orders.

17. As the deacon and his wife evolve into a couple whose union is defined by mutual love-become-service, his ability to witness the servanthood of Christ to the Church is perfected. Their marital union becomes a genuine source of grace for his diaconate.

18. Much of what has been said cannot obviously take place unless the wife of the deacon, and by natural extension his children, understand and value the ministry to which their husband and father commits himself by ordination, and also know and accept how that commitment will change his life and theirs.

19. The Church is obliged to assist the wife of a deacon in appreciating how important she is in the design of God, a design that has placed her husband within apostolic ministry.

20. The joy a deacon's wife knows through their mutual growth in love-become-service must become one with the Church's joy in receiving her husband's gift of himself. Their joy becomes all the greater as she gives birth with her husband to a new witness to that same love in his diaconal ministry.

21. Becoming a deacon's wife not only leads to joy, but will also ask of her a certain self-denial. She will always need to be present to her husband, but presence takes many forms, and knowing how to choose among them in the varied moments of his ministry will always be her challenge.

22. It is incumbent upon the Church to provide for the deacon's wife's formation, in an appropriate way that is distinct from her husband's, and particular to her own needs.

23. From the first days of Aspirancy to her husband's retirement from assigned ministry, a deacon's wife needs be made aware of all commitments that oblige him, especially those formally made through agreements of service.

24. The Church is responsible to help the deacon's children, especially the younger ones, to experience the newness of their father's ministry and their parent's commitment as an enrichment of their family life and its bonds.

25. The inclusion of the life witness of the married couple within the diaconal mission is clearly a major expansion of what being a deacon means for most people. The married deacon is actually performing diaconal ministry as he and his wife live the day-to-day realities of a married couple, committed to fulfilling their union in love-become-service.

26. The presence of diaconal married couples in the midst of the Church community is a service, rendered in the form of encouragement, not only to married couples but also to all who are engaged in family life ministries.

Some Personal Thoughts on Achieving Integration

I have always thought that a well-articulated theory is of itself eminently practical. As a teacher of homiletics, for example, I am convinced that poor preaching is commonly rooted in a lack of understanding of what a homily is supposed to do and what a homilist is supposed to be. Get the theory right and you clearly increase your odds of preaching a good homily. However, my teaching experience has also convinced me that many people do not appreciate how understanding drives action, and consequently don't see the connection. What I regularly taught in my theology courses as the requisite understanding for an effective spiritual or pastoral practice, my students often characterized as abstract and of little long-term import. Yet, as I remember it, there were always some in whose eyes you could read the excitement as their minds raced towards previously unimagined applications. While I hope that the readers of my present essay intuit a useful application as readily, I will offer a few personal thoughts, should some among them be grateful for any indication of how the desired integration might be achievable in practice.

- *Can you see the connection between knowing what something is and what it's supposed to do and then using it really well? Give an example of your own.*

- *What does the aphorism "understanding drives action" mean to you? Do you believe it's universally true?*

I am neither a permanent deacon nor a married man. Consequently, my observations are made from outside the lived reality upon which I have ventured to reflect. However, I do believe there are sufficient parallels between the integration the married deacon seeks and the integration I have strived for in my priesthood. What I can offer here are some insights from my own experience that might prove helpful to a diaconal couple seeking a more directly practical application of the vision elaborated in my essay. As I said at the outset, I view all of this as no more than a hopefully legitimate and substantive beginning of a deeper appreciation of the interplay of the two sacraments that a married deacon and his wife must live and fulfill. What comes of my thoughts will be decided by the diaconal couples who may happen to reflect upon them.

- *Do you believe that someone could offer useful insights from personal experience to others whose lives are clearly quite different?*

- *What common elements in all our lives bind us together?*

I remember, from the twenty years I both taught in a seminary and served as a member of the formation team, how often individual seminarians professed to be overwhelmed by the demands made upon them. On the whole,

I never questioned their sincerity. They were expected to achieve reasonable success in a professional degree program. They served in a pastoral placement for a full day once a week. They were expected to participate fully in the daily liturgical life of the Church and develop as well a personal spiritual and prayer life. We regularly challenged their human development, more often by accenting their shortcomings rather than by applauding their accomplishments. And, of course, they needed their downtime, for rest and recreation, for exercise and social needs.

• *Can you see anything of yourself in this mirror? What is it?*

I speak of this from my time in priestly service in a seminary, rather than from my own time of formation. The seminary I entered was a regimented world in which you learned to do what you were expected to do. Most of us did that, even though we regularly lamented our lot among ourselves. No one, as I recall, ever told us how to hold it all together. The only piece of advice I do remember came from a professor who contrasted two types of seminaries. There was the Sulpician seminary, where, when you came and said you wanted to be a priest, they replied, "We will help you." Then there was, according to him, the Roman seminary, where, when you said you wanted to be a priest, they retorted, "Prove it." He then, with an all too obvious morose chuckle, added, "Gentlemen, this is not a Sulpician seminary." And so I never really learned how to integrate, but I did learn how to survive.

I do have to confess, however, that I was never really much aware of any particularly burdensome difficulty in holding it all together. Academic success came easy to me, and, for the rest, my natural easy-going temperament served me well. I eventually finished my seminary studies and formation at an Italian seminary in Rome, where I did discover that, for whatever reasons, one out of every two of us Americans, who shared the same common experience, could not adjust to the added demands of a transition to a foreign culture. These left the seminary and moved on, some to priestly studies elsewhere, but most not. As kind and hospitable as Italians can be, I still found no clear guidance given for the integration of the elements of my life.

- *Do you ever feel that you're just surviving, barely holding it together? Do you honestly feel that there must be a better way? Share your feelings with each other.*

- *Have you had any real guidance from anyone in your life on integrating the many elements of it? Individually? As a couple? How well has it served you?*

These were the years of the Second Vatican Council. Priestly ministry and life, and seminary formation as well, were openly part of the conciliar discussion and debate. Integration in ministry was becoming part of the Church's professed agenda. The issue was taken up explicitly in regard to priests in the last session of the Council in 1965. Promulgated in October, the *Decree on Priestly Formation* presented a unified vision of priestly formation centered on Jesus Christ, and specifically on Christ, the Good Shepherd. Every program of instruction was now to be directed toward the goal of readying men for the ministry of a shepherd. Two months later, the *Decree on the Ministry and Life of Priests* returned to the shepherd image to describe the interface between the priesthood and the world.

While the ministry of Christ forbids the priest to conform
to the world, it also requires that he live in the world
among men.

It is at this juncture that the Council began to unfold
the shepherd imagery, based upon Jesus' description of the
Model Shepherd in the Gospel of John, chapter ten. The
love of the good shepherd for his sheep drives his need to
know them, his willingness to lay down his life for them,
and his acknowledgement that there are others beyond the
fold. The same shepherd image is explicitly linked to the
unity of life of the priest, the integration issue, in number
fourteen of the decree. The unity of life is to be found in
the imitation of Christ, again specifically in imitation of the
Model Shepherd. "...Christ forever remains the source
and origin of their unity of life. Therefore priests attain to
the unity of their lives by uniting themselves with Christ in
acknowledging the Father's will and in the gift of themselves on behalf of the flock committed to them. Thus, by
assuming the role of the Good Shepherd, they will find in
the very exercise of pastoral love the bond of priestly perfection which will unify their lives and activities." Pastoral
love, shepherd love, is the integrating principle.

Blessed John Paul II unfailingly returned to the unifying image of the Good Shepherd and the integrating
power of pastoral charity whenever he addressed the
priests of the Church. At the very beginning of his pontifi-
cate, his 1979 *Holy Thursday Letter* developed the Good
Shepherd theme to define a priestly vocation as "a singular
solicitude for the salvation of our neighbor." It was in this
solicitude that he challenged the priest to find the meaning
and full significance of his life.

In 1992, John Paul gave us his definitive reflection on
the priesthood, and most specifically on the interface
between the priest and the world, in *I Will Give You*

Shepherds, his post-synodal apostolic exhortation of the
formation of priests in the circumstances of the present
day. In the midst of a developed and lengthy reflection, he
forcefully asserted that "...pastoral charity is the dynamic
inner principle capable of unifying the many different
activities of the priest. In virtue of this pastoral charity the
essential and permanent demand for unity between the
priest's interior life and all his external actions and the
obligations of the ministry can be properly fulfilled, a
demand particularly urgent in a socio-cultural and ecclesial
context marked by complexity, fragmentation and disper-
sion. Only by directing every moment and every one of
his acts towards the fundamental choice to 'give his life for
the flock' can the priest guarantee this unity which is vital
and indispensable for his harmony and spiritual balance."
I doubt that it can be better said. We had finally arrived at
an explicit articulation of the wisdom that, from the beginning, had given the good priest his interior peace and
integrity of life.

• *"The unity of life is found in the imitation of
Christ..." Why do you think Christians must ulti-
mately find the answer to their lives' needs in Jesus
Christ?*

• *Why do you think the Church turned to the shepherd
image to describe the ministry and life of the priest?*

• *Can you see a connection between imitating the Good
Shepherd and developing the kind of love that could
successfully integrate the whole of a priest's life?*

• *It would seem that a kind of love appropriate to a person's life situation is the key to a successful integration of life. Do you agree? Why? If not, why not?*

I was in the seminary in Rome during that last session of the Council. Ordained in 1970, I began my twenty years in seminary teaching and formation in 1972. It was in those early years that I began to relate explicitly to the Good Shepherd imagery and to pastoral charity as an integrating principle, in my own need to unify my life, and in my responsibility to help the young men in priestly formation to do the same. Here is what I learned.

First of all, an image is necessary. Images, unlike mere concepts, enable us to address the deeper elements of our own interiority. Concepts do speak to the mind, and that is good and indeed necessary for clarity of thought and communication. Images go through the mind and speak ultimately to the often unfathomable recesses of our hearts. We think thoughts, but we feel images. In 1970, when I was ordained, I had in place the right thoughts about the priesthood. What I didn't have yet in place was the feeling of the priesthood, an affective appropriation of its reality that would prove eventually necessary to guide my decision-making and to unify my life. Now I'm not saying I wasn't holding it together. I had learned to do that in the seminary and, as I said, I was never particularly burdened in my attempts to do so. However, there is a radical difference between holding it together, which comes from one's own strength, and experiencing the unity of life through a power that ultimately comes as a gift from another. Merely holding it together does not achieve integration, it just keeps you out of trouble. It is like throwing a lot of ingredients into a pot, which, unless heat is applied, never become a soup. The heat comes from the image; or, more accurately, from the reality the image invites us to imitate.

- *I hope that you had the right thoughts about Christian marriage when you exchanged vows. When did you come to possess the feeling of your marriage as Christian, affectively appropriating its goals and values as your own? How did that happen? If it hasn't really happened for you, why not?*

- *Can you see the power of an image in helping us come to the right feeling about our lives and their particular situations? Are there any images that you have already invoked for guidance and strength in your life? Individually? As a couple?*

- *"...there is a radical difference between holding it together, which comes from one's own strength, and experiencing the unity of life through a power that ultimately comes as a gift from another." Have you experienced anything like this already in your life? Share your memories and then give thanks for the gift.*

- *How might a deeper appreciation of this enhance your witness as a Christian married couple? As a married diaconal couple?*

This leads me to the second lesson I learned. The image must be actively engaged and imitated. My own appreciation of the image of the Good Shepherd, as presented by John in the tenth chapter of his gospel, has focused on three fundamental behaviors that characterize the good shepherd and constitute pastoral charity.

First of all, the shepherd's voice is recognized by the sheep. To pursue pastoral charity actively I had to ensure that, whatever the circumstances, my voice, my address in all its aspects, was always recognizable as genuinely compassionate, no matter whom I was addressing and what message I had. All pastoral care and, in fact, all evangelization begin with an act of solidarity, modeled on the Word become flesh, for us and for our salvation.

Secondly, the true shepherd willingly lays down his life for his sheep. Pastoral charity is an exercise in self-forgetfulness that evokes in its beneficiary both personal worth and authentic hope. It is an act of compassionate extravagance, modeled on the Crucified Savior, who loved us and handed himself over for our sake. I had to learn to shape my behavior, no longer by the canons of self-interest, but by the law of Christ. I admit that this particular imitation is difficult and needs daily recommitment. I have also learned, however, that even small successes in laying down your life for another leave a long lasting and energizing residue in your heart.

Finally, the good shepherd draws no boundaries beyond which his care does not extend. There are always other sheep. Pastoral charity then is a continual outreach that embraces willingly whoever is in need. It imitates Jesus, whose earthly ministry was ordinarily directed to the most needy individual, the little one, who emerged before him from the crowd. In one sense, this aspect is easier than the other two. More often than not I found the one who needed compassion standing relatively nearby. I have come to include regularly in my prayer my own need for the eyes of Christ, that, whatever room or space I might enter, I would always find the one person most in need of presence, affirmation, and care.

If you merge these three fundamental behaviors, they form together a clear image of the love of the Good

Shepherd, the integrating love that enables priests to attain to the unity of their lives. Imitating these three behaviors consistently in all relationships and actively pursuing them as a defining habit, a priest can live a full and varied life without any compromise to his identity and mission. In fact, it is his effective desire to be one with their common point of origin in the heart of Christ that joins a man's being a priest to his affectivity, thus moving him from possibly a merely valid priesthood to an abundantly fruitful one.

- *Can you see how a scriptural image can provide a set of imitable behaviors for someone whose life situation relates to that particular image? What do you think of this as a tool for integration?*

- *As a Catholic, do the behaviors indicated above provide in your mind proper guidance for a man seeking to be a good priest? Do you know any priests whose lives appear to be based upon such a pattern of behaviors? Consider having a conversation with one of them about this.*

- *Do all the faithful need this witness of pastoral charity to help them in their own life's journey and discipleship? Why?*

- *What have you learned about God and about yourself through the presence in your life of priests whose lives are true witnesses to pastoral charity?*

AN IMAGE FOR THE
MARRIED PERMANENT DEACON

Now, if I am correct in identifying love-become-service as the practical form the divine love assumes in sacramental union with the Christian married couple, and consequently as the heart of the self-gift that a married permanent deacon brings to his ministry as a sacramental sign in the Church of the servanthood of Jesus Christ, then discerning the image that most powerfully merges all these elements is the first step in unifying a permanent deacon's life. May I suggest that there is no more telling image of love-become-service than that of Jesus rising from table on the night before he died and washing the feet of his disciples? While this image pales before Jesus' ultimate demonstration of love-become-service on the cross, it serves as a more accessible model of the behaviors that the permanent deacon and his wife can daily engage and imitate in pursuit of unity in their marriage and ministry.

As the priest finds in the image of the Good Shepherd the integrating love that enables him to attain unity in his life, the diaconal couple is invited to look to the image of the Foot-washer to discover the Christ-like behaviors of which they are most in need. The same Gospel of Saint John that models for us the pastoral charity of the Good Shepherd also models the behaviors of Jesus the Servant in the Last Supper narrative.

"...He rose from supper and took off his outer garments. He took a towel and tied it around his waist. Then he poured water into a basin and began to wash the disciples' feet and dry them with the towel around his waist. He came to Simon Peter, who said to him, 'Master, are you going to wash my feet?' Jesus answered and said to him, 'What I am doing you do not understand now, but you will understand later.' Peter said to him, 'You will never wash my feet.' Jesus answered him, 'Unless I wash you, you will have no inheritance with me.' ...when he had washed their feet, and put his garments back on and reclined at table again, he said to them, 'Do you realize what I have done for you? You call me teacher and master, and rightly so, for indeed I am. If I, therefore, the master and teacher, have washed your feet, you ought to wash one another's feet. I have given you a model to follow, so that as I have done for you, you should also do.' " (John 13: 4-8, 12-15).

- *Had you been at table with Peter and the others, how would you have reacted to Jesus' wanting to wash your feet? Would your relationship with him have taken on a new dimension because of what he did?*

- *Why do you think he wanted his disciples also to become foot-washers?*

• *Pastors wash the feet of twelve parishioners on Holy Thursday. What impact do you think that has on a parish community?*

• *How have you, as husband and wife, washed each other's feet?*

The scriptural narrative describing the washing of the disciples' feet at the Last Supper recalls five specific behaviors modeled by Jesus at that moment. His service to his disciples begins as he rises from the table. Although he rightfully presides at the supper, he moves away from his proper place, from its prestige and its claim that it is he who ought to be served. Guided by that image, the love that seeks to become service in Christian marriage begins its journey in a movement away from a self concerned with position and prerogatives. It renounces all calculation in the shaping of relationship and common life. It never says, "You owe me," to the other. In fact, I suspect, there is nothing more lethal to a successful marriage than a heart that is fixated on maintaining its perceived rightful share of authority and prestige, as based on some predetermined calculation, whether fifty-fifty or otherwise. The only love that can ever become the kind of service that bonds two lives into one is the love that willingly forgets self for the sake of the beloved. It is the love with which God loves us. It is the love that grace empowers in the Christian married couple. The baptized husband and wife best begin their journey toward unity by mutually determining to imitate the Jesus "who rose from supper and took off his outer garments," the symbols of his status. Love-become-service begins in an act of renunciation and self-forgetfulness.

• Have you ever approached your marriage as a fifty-fifty proposition, or some other calculated division of responsibility? How has that worked for you?

• Do you believe marriage is meant to be more than a contract? How so? What does that do to your approach as a couple to responsibilities and tasks?

• Have you been selfless for the sake of your spouse? How does that work itself out in day-to-day life?

• How might a Christian married couple "rise from supper and take off their outer garments" in imitation of Jesus?

The second behavior modeled by Jesus follows directly upon the first, as self-forgetfulness practically begins to address the needs of the other. Jesus takes the towel and the basin into his own hands. He does not direct another to do what must be done. He himself takes up what is needed. The transformation of love into service is a hands-on project. Beginning in renunciation, it is a true spiritual poverty that is so empty of self that nothing that helps the other is beneath it. Declarations of limits, as in the clichéd "I don't do windows," effectively abort the journey into unity and true mutuality of life. Whatever must be done is willingly and directly done, for such again is the love that saves us, the love that transforms mere human love into a sacrament. Imitating the poverty of love, as they see it in the hands that take up the towel and basin, will move a husband and wife ever closer to their becoming here on earth a bright witness to the divine love itself, and to the fulfillment of their marriage.

• *Have you set any limits to what you will or will not do for your spouse? For your children and family?*

• *Have you set any limits to your willingness to forgive? If you have, what are they and how do you justify them in a Christian marriage?*

• *How have you already in your marriage "taken up a towel and basin" for the sake of your spouse?*

• *What might happen to a marriage in which the spouses forgot the message of "the towel and the basin?"*

The third behavior is really part of the second. This spiritually poor hands-on love is given, over and over again, in the ordinary living of our daily lives. Jesus washes feet that have become dusty from travel and dirty in their daily use. He dries them with an easy but clearly perceptible tenderness. The service rendered in itself is not particularly spectacular, nor notable. What is extraordinary is that he, who is in no way personally obliged, gladly performs it. We say, "You didn't have to do that," and he responds with a caring smile, "I know." Attentiveness to ordinary everyday needs, no matter how insignificant, how easily overlooked, is a telling demonstration of the sincerity and authenticity of love. Showing love consistently in the little things of life is not only an undeniable strengthening of the bond between a husband and wife, it is a true imitation of the humility of Christ. It becomes a life-transforming holiness.

• *How have you seen love revealed in attentiveness to ordinary everyday needs? A meal needing to be made... Kids needing to be picked up... A widowed parent needing you around... An extra trip to the food market for a forgotten item... A hand needing to be held... Share some examples from your own experience?*

• *Do you have any everyday needs that your spouse seems to overlook? Be honest and tender as you share your thoughts and feelings on this.*

• *How willing are you as a couple to do for each other and for others "what you really don't have to do?"*

• *How is this a true God-likeness, a true "holiness?"*

The fourth and the fifth behaviors of Jesus' foot-washing reveal two essential qualities that accompany love-become-service, of which the first is patience. Peter doesn't understand why Jesus has risen from table and is washing his feet. He sees the service, but he has yet to understand the fullness of the love. We have here a faint echo of Peter's far more serious failures to understand Jesus, failures on the road to Jerusalem, in the garden of Gethsemane, and at the Sea of Tiberias after the Resurrection. Then as now, Jesus accepts Peter with his lack of understanding, but assures him that a day will come, when he will understand what Jesus is doing for him.

Even in the most intimate of relationships, the individuals that are in them are unique. Walking a common path towards unity of life in Christian marriage does not mean that the two, however committed to one another, will understand the full import of the other's actions at any given moment. Even the most beloved do not grow in spiritual understanding and transformation at the same pace. Husbands and wives have to learn how to walk together.

Jesus does not require that what he does for us be fully grasped at the moment. He allows the unfolding of life to reveal to us what indeed is occurring. He is very patient with Peter, and with us. Our imitation of him then calls for a long-endured patience that is at peace, even when misunderstood or wrongfully judged. It is a patience born out of absolute trust in the transforming power of love. Like the imperfect community of believers at Corinth, the Christian married couple must learn to receive each other, not only at the Table of the Lord, but daily in the present moment of their lives. They must learn to wait for one another.

- *Have you ever misunderstood or misinterpreted your spouse's love for you? Was he or she hurt by that? How did you respond?*

- *Has your spouse ever misunderstood your attempts at love and care? How did you move beyond your frustration at not being understood?*

- *Do you have the patience "to wait for one another" and "to learn how to walk together?" How have you accomplished this in your marriage? Are you still in need of learning these things?*

Closely allied with patience is persistence, a conscious resolve to remain steadfast in self-forgetfulness and self-gift for the sake of the beloved. Peter's proud and defensive outburst, "You will never wash my feet," does not deter Jesus. He does not accept the finality of Peter's caring but thoughtless words. "Fine! If that's what you want..." He does not restrain his love and forego the service, which his love desires to perform and which Peter professes not to need. Jesus persists, allowing both the reality of the need and the urgency of his love to overcome the foolish pride that resists being served. He teaches Peter, and indeed all of us, that authentic being-together must include a joyful willingness to be served as well as to serve.

The persistence then of love-becoming-service does not overwhelm, nor seek a forced acceptance. That would be domination, a manipulative distortion of love, which in the end would destroy all mutuality and unity. Rather, it seeks to reveal the true dignity inherent in being-served. Allowing another to love us, to do us good, even in things we could easily do for ourselves, arises out of an awareness of the importance of mutual reciprocity in achieving true unity and harmony in our human relationships. Love cannot become service unless another loving heart is willing to be served.

- *How do you feel if your gestures of attention and love are resisted by your spouse, or even rejected? Have you ever felt the temptation to give up, either in life or in marriage?*

- *How great must love become for it to be able to endure all things and persist in its offer of goodness and care? Where do you turn to find such strength?*

- *Deacons and their wives are often very active in church and community service. Has it ever been difficult for you to allow others to do for you? Share some memories of such times. In the end, what did you do?*

• *How important to a marriage is it to allow your spouse to serve you? What is the best response?*

Imitation of Jesus, the foot-washer, in Christian marriage involves both husband and wife in a continual dynamism of giving and receiving, the elements of which, I suspect, will be intrinsically inseparable throughout the course of their lives. However, as evidenced by Peter, this does not preclude their need to awaken to this reality and to accept humbly its exigency. There will be foolish moments when pride may cause one of them to stumble, when the remnants of spiritual isolation will prompt declarations of self-sufficiency. It is in such moments that the love that seeks to serve must remember the gentle persistence of Jesus that found a way to remind Peter of why his being-served was so important. The Christian married couple that places this particular exchange between Jesus and Peter within the heart of their own life conversation will find themselves well on the way to a lasting and life-giving unity.

• *Has your pride ever gotten in the way of the love between you and your spouse? Talk about it with each other.*

• *What virtues and attitudes do you think are necessary for a married couple to continually "wash each other's feet?"*

• *How might you gently remind each other of what is mutually necessary to fulfill the potential of a truly Christian marriage?*

Love-become-service, as modeled upon the image of Jesus' washing the feet of his disciples, begins in an act of renunciation of prestige and proper place. A hands-on project, it is a spiritual poverty that is so empty of self that nothing that helps the other is beneath it. It gives itself, over and over again, in the ordinary living of daily life. It is both patient and persistent. Trusting in the transformative power of love, it can wait without anxiety for the other to catch up in understanding and appreciation. It knows how to overcome an all too common resistance to being served, so that both giving and receiving are treasured and enjoyed. All of this is spoken to us by the image of Jesus, the foot-washer. "I have given you a model to follow, so that as I have done for you, you should also do."

- *With Jesus this is a package deal. How is what he shows us truly wonderful and so much needed in our lives? If you're excited by this and want this more deeply as part of your love for each other, now is the time to share your thoughts and commit to it in prayer together before God.*

- *As a package deal, it's a lot. It's also then an awesome and fearful thing to imitate. It is not going to be an easy path. Share your hesitations and encourage one another. This is a good time for a long and quiet embrace.*

AN INTEGRATING IMAGE
AND PRINCIPLE FOR THE DIACONATE

Thus far, in reflecting on the behaviors evidenced by Jesus in washing the feet of his disciples, I have limited my observations to the impact of that image on the life of the Christian married couple. My contention is that the image of the foot-washer, as it illustrates authentic love-become-service, is the most appropriate integrating image, not only for Christian marriage, but uniquely for the married permanent deacon. This requires some further reflection on its application to diaconal ministry.

Our Catholic theology of the diaconate fundamentally understands the deacon as signing the servanthood of Jesus Christ. While that servanthood finds its origin in the Mystery of the Incarnation and its fulfillment in the Paschal Mystery, there is perhaps no more universally applicable demonstration of it than in the foot-washing at the Last Supper. As faithful members of the Body of Christ, we can so readily become one with the Christ of the Incarnation and of the Paschal Mystery by becoming one through imitation with the Christ of the foot-washing. As Church we are called to daily put on Jesus Christ, to be conformed to him. It is his law that lives in us and liberates us. A spirituality of servant-hood must animate our common Christian vocation in whatever form it is lived. Signing that servanthood is the greatest gift the deacon gives to the Church and to the individual faithful. The deacon who makes the behaviors of the foot-washer the integrating behaviors of his own life stimulates and guides the people toward the fulfillment of their own identity in union with Jesus Christ. However, for this witness to emerge powerfully in the life of the Church a certain correction of some common understandings needs to be undertaken.

- *Do you believe the average Catholic values the imitation of Christ as a personal priority? If yes, how do you see that happening? If not, why not?*

- *Has the imitation of Christ been an integral part of your own spiritual journey? What particular aspects of Christ have you tried to imitate? In what kind of situations? As spouses, share this part of your story with each other.*

- *Do you think that imitating the behaviors of the foot-washing is the key in any believer's life to the daily putting-on of Jesus Christ?*

The Fathers of the Second Vatican Council had recourse to the tripartite appreciation, common to both Protestant and Catholic theology since the Reformation, of the person and work of Christ as Teacher, Priest, and Shepherd, to illumine the offices and responsibilities of both the laity and the ordained. Since then the understanding of the deacon as someone called to a particular consecration to the ministry of the Word, of the Altar, and of Charity has been universally received and today shapes even such mundane applications as service agreements. While most expositions of diaconal ministry list several specific activities under each of these headings, most conclude by focusing on the ministry of Charity as the deacon's most practical ministry, and, at least by inference, his most proper one.

- *How do you think that the average person-in-the-pew views the work of deacons? In their eyes, what are deacons supposed to do?*

- *As an ordained deacon, what do you think deacons should be doing above all else?*

This arises, I believe, from an all too quick and practically exclusive turn to the narrative in Acts 6: 1-6, which has the Apostles, in need of assistants to care for the needs of the widows of the Greek-speaking community, praying and laying hands on seven chosen men. The common use of the text in magisterial documents and as a reading in the Rite of Ordination of Deacons certainly has given its very visual emphasis of waiting on tables a dominant influence in our theological and pastoral understandings of the diaconate. However, it is only one source of understanding, and should not therefore unilaterally determine our ultimate concretization of the sacramentality of the diaconate. In fact, if the servanthood of Christ, of which the deacon exists as a sign, were effectively reduced, in the perception of both pastors and people alike, to individual and specific works of charity, then I would argue that a grave loss had been suffered by the Church. The servanthood of Christ is part of a salvific mystery that far exceeds charitable works as such. As it cannot be defined by them, so neither can the ministry of a deacon.

My point here parallels what I had said earlier in this essay regarding the listing of God, wife, family, work, and ministry, as a prioritizing tool in the life of the married permanent deacon. Prioritizing compartmentalizes rather than integrates. It can easily produce unintended tensions and disappointments where there ought not to be any. If the three evocations of diaconal ministry are viewed as separate concerns, as three separable groupings of related tasks, then our human inclination to categorize and rank will almost unreflectively begin to order them from most important to least. And so we view with at least veiled disapproval those deacons who apparently seek merely to serve in the sanctuary. And we applaud and encourage those others whose ministerial time is almost completely taken up with soup kitchens and other such similar services. But is one form of service ever more important than another? Can a deacon ever rightly give himself to one so exclusively as to minimize his involvement in the others? Are the three not in fact one, articulated in a variety of situations across the full spectrum of human need?

- *It's easy to see how working in a soup kitchen, organizing a clothing drive, addressing the needs of the homebound, and the like, are true services. Performed by a deacon, they sign the servanthood of Christ. How is the deacon's ministry of the Word also a true service of human need?*

- *How is his ministry of the Altar a true service to human need as well?*

- *Are you personally more comfortable serving in any one of these ministries as opposed to the other two? How might this become a problem?*

• *How might prioritizing these three actually result in a distortion of the servanthood of Jesus Christ?*

It's useful at this point to remember that this trifold distinction of ministerial tasks was first employed during the Reformation as a way for us to focus on the person of Christ in his salvific relationship to us. The Protestant "Prophet, Priest, and King" and the Catholic "Priest, Prophet, and King" were never anything more than a finite attempt at a categorization of the benefits and blessings that we acknowledge to be ours in and through Jesus Christ, whose identity and ministry are ultimately ineffable and infinite. Simply put, the three categories do not exhaust the mystery of the Incarnate Son of God. They are useful for us to praise our Lord for what he does for us, and to order our own response to him, but the sum of them is not the totality of his person and work. They therefore are neither separable nor exhaustive of who he is and what he does for us. In the light of that, I would argue that what is true in the original instance of the use of this model remains true in all instances of its use.

The deacon who serves Christ, Teacher, Priest, and Shepherd, in the Ministry of the Word, of the Altar, and of Charity, serves a mystery that ultimately defies categorization. Any specific task he takes up in any of these ministries is rooted in an indivisible whole, and therefore can never be played off for importance against any other. He is defined then by no specific task or area of concern. His identity must find its origin deeper within the Mystery of the Incarnate Son, in a dimension of it that is coextensive with Christ's identity and inseparable from it. Our Catholic tradition has consistently identified that point of origin with the form assumed by the Eternal Son in the Incarnation, the form proclaimed in Philippians (2: 6-8) as the form of a slave, a humble emptying of self even unto death on a cross. Did not Jesus himself identify that point of origin to his contentious disciples when he disabused them of their narcissistic and divisive attempts at ranking by his humbling words, "I am in your midst as one who serves."? (Luke 22: 27)

- *Do you think that Jesus' self-description, "I am in your midst as one who serves," is applicable to each and every aspect of his ministry and life? If so, share some examples of this from the Gospels. If not, why not?*

- *The servanthood of Christ, while certainly about what he does, is ultimately more about who he is. While what you do as a married couple is good and important, is it not true that in the end it's more about who you are? Talk about this for a while.*

- *Is this true also of us as individuals?*

- *We are always more than the sum of our works. True or false? Why?*

And so the deacon serves Christ, Teacher, Priest, and Shepherd in the Ministry of the Word, of the Altar, and of Charity. We use this language because it's very useful and reasonably traditional. It's intellectually satisfying to organize the many vocations of the People of God and unite them to their source in Jesus Christ by the use of a single analytical model. In every case, however, an all pervasive and transcendent principle of harmony and unity needs to be affirmed. The priest, called to sign the holiness of Christ, integrates his life through pastoral charity. The

Christian married couple, called to sign the fidelity, the permanence, and the generativity of God, integrates its common life by love-become-service. The deacon is called to sign the servant form of Christ, and to do so in all that he does. He integrates his life through the same self-emptying service that characterizes the entire mystery of the person and work of Jesus Christ.

Tasks as apparently diverse as teaching a religious education class, assisting at a Sunday Mass, and grilling hot dogs at a parish picnic, when performed by a deacon, speak to the Church community of how we are to interface with the world, because of how God became one with us in Jesus Christ. Rooted in a deacon's very being and expressive of his fundamental commitment, anything and everything that he does become capable of faithful witness to Christ. A particular action is predetermined as diaconal not by the stuff it engages but by the humility that moves the deacon to take it up and by the compassion that moves him to direct it to another's need.

- *Two men are grilling hot dogs at a parish picnic. One is deacon, the other is not. What's the difference?*

- *Does the service define the deacon, or does the deacon define the service? Explain.*

This is not meant to deny that certain services rendered to the Church, because of custom or context, are readily identified by the community as diaconal. This is apparent for the services that spread the Word of God, that assist at the Eucharistic sacrifice, that care for the poor, the sick, and all who are in need. These services become what we call "ministries," official, structured, and expected. However valid and necessary such formal ministries are, they do not exhaust the servanthood whose living sign the deacon has become. All is service when rendered by a humble and compassionate man transformed by the laying on of hands and the power of the Holy Spirit.

- *How does service become a ministry? Can you give an example from your own community or parish experience?*

- *What is the difference in the witness given to the servanthood of Jesus Christ through incidental acts and through formal ministries?*

THE UNION OF THE INTEGRATING PRINCIPLES IN ONE AND THE SAME CHRIST

Love-become-service in Christian marriage and self-emptying-service in the diaconate have a common origin in the self-communication of God to the human person. This self-gift, made in the power of the Spirit and in the image of the Word, moves from the creation of the human person in the image and likeness of God to the perfecting of the same through the death and the resurrection of Jesus Christ. Man, in all aspects of his life and at every moment of his story, is intimately bound up with the mystery of personhood, which inextricably links him to God. From his first days to his last he is addressed by the Word and shaped by the Spirit.

- *How do you understand "personhood?" Or put another way, what makes a person a "person." What's the difference between a "person" and a "thing?"*

The "adam," the one called forth in the beginning from the earth, was made a person, a being whose purpose is to love and whose perfection is the fulfillment of that vocation.

Called into personhood, the human being was made for a unique relationship with God. Its destiny was to find perfection and self-fulfillment in an act of love towards the One who loved it into existence. For a created and therefore limited being, however, learning how to love perfectly is a precarious task, a journey subject to many possible missteps. And so God, never absent, mercifully and continually provided needed assistance through many and varied graces. Of the many favors bestowed upon us, two emerge as definitive to the story of every human person. One responds to our original limitation, our solitude, and the other to our eventual failures, our sinfulness. Both have been given us through one and the same Christ, the firstborn of all creation and the firstborn from the dead.

- *Do you agree with the assertion that learning how to love perfectly is difficult for us?*

- *God's entire involvement with us is about teaching us how to love perfectly. Do you agree or disagree? Explain.*

Consider the first favor, our true first blessing. Oriented toward a perfect union in love between self and God, a human being could never intuit the way as a solitary. And so God made the "adam" both male and female. Their relationship, one to the other, through the many travails of our fragile earthly life, was so designed from its beginning to be a kind of school in which we as persons would learn of our undeniable need for love and test our first expressions of it. Their eventual union, perfected through Christ, would form them according to the heart of the divine love itself. Their restless hearts could now embrace in Christ the One for whose love they were made.

Begun in the light of the eternal and creative Word, their journey toward an authentic and perfect love would come to completion in the grace of the incarnate Word, Jesus Christ. The Word that first named them and called them forth is one and the same Word that is the Lord, who in the fullness of time has made their love an image of his love for his Church. He gave us the final shaping of our interpersonal vocation as he empowered us through his Spirit to live and love, male and female, in a faithful, permanent, and life-giving way.

A man and a woman fulfill their human vocation as their love for one another, through Christ, becomes a free and total gift of self to the other, as love becomes service. Only love of this kind can worthily be offered to the One who first loved us into being. They fulfill their baptismal vocation as they witness this particular love before the world. Christian marriage is part of the grace of Jesus Christ, who is the Father's most perfective and perfect grace given the human person, the one being in all of creation who in turn was made purposefully for God. Christian marriage is the fulfillment in the fullness of time of the initial grace bestowed on the "adam." The solitary one, whom God then made male and female, has learned how to love, and has become one again in Jesus Christ.

- *How is the Genesis account of the creation of human persons already oriented toward Christian sacramental marriage?*

- *How does Christian marriage advance the plan of God for the human person?*

• Do you believe that Christian marriage to fulfill itself must be lived as a covenant between husband, wife, and Jesus Christ? If so, why? Have you been successful in including Jesus in your marriage? If not, why not?

This first blessing of being male and female, this first divine favor, would perhaps have sufficed, had we not found a way to deform it. We were created for love, but also made with freedom, for without freedom a gift cannot be given, love cannot exist. In that primal freedom, however aware we were of our call to intimacy with God, how ill-disposed we were, like petulant children, to hear the word "no," even when spoken by our loving Creator. How obsessed we could become in our desire to possess what clearly was not ours. How full of self we were to even think of becoming like gods. How manipulative we could be in drawing into our own deluded vision the partner we should have only loved. "...And they both ate of the fruit of the tree..." However much we say the serpent tricked us, we cannot shift the blame, for temptation cannot of itself bring about sin.

• Why is it that children often have such a problem with the word "no?" Do you still have a problem with it?

• Might this problem with the word "no" be part of the ongoing expression of humanity's original sin?

• How have you, as a married couple, dealt with "no" in your marriage relationship?

Ironically, made for love and aching for it, our human story became a chronicle of manipulation and abuse, of violence and destruction. Unable to love God with a spontaneous and heartfelt affection, we dug for ourselves, in the words of the prophet Jeremiah, "cisterns, broken cisterns, that hold no water." We spent our lives, and indeed those of others, searching for a panacea for our broken hearts, only to discover that it was not within our power to heal the wound we had inflicted upon ourselves. At the core of our being, however, we remained interwoven with the self-disclosure of God, within the common mystery of our shared personhood. Dead in our sin we became the beneficiaries of an unexpected and clearly unmerited favor. The Word of God became one of us.

- *Saint Anselm believed that original sin as we experience it is primarily our loss of a spontaneous and affective love for God. Do you see that in your own experience of sin?*

- *Why do you think we cannot heal ourselves?*

The incarnation of the eternal Word became not only the final and definitive revelation of God but also led us back to our own true selves and forward to our ultimate perfection. Jesus Christ not only reveals God to us, but reveals us to ourselves. In his person and work, we see again the "adam," the one created for love of God. He shows us with greater clarity than ever the immensity of the Father's love for us, and embraces us in its power. In him we see the truth, how we can be free from the power of sin and rise to an authentic love of God. Being loved and forgiven by Jesus, we begin to fall in love with God. He is our new Adam, and in him we are born again.

• *Jesus said, "To see me is to see the Father." What then does God look like?*

• *Saint Paul calls Jesus Christ, "the new Adam." How does the story of the new humanity begun in and through Jesus differ from that of the old humanity?*

Jesus loved us and handed himself over, over to the cross, the product of everything that was wrong with us. Through his self-gift, he made it the tree of life. And of its fruit we were invited to eat in abundance. We left our broken cisterns and followed him, eating and drinking at his table, caught up in the transforming power of a wondrously deep and abiding affection for God. We wept like Peter, and again, like Peter, we rejoiced and went forth in boldness. Jesus had emptied himself for our sake, and, together with him, we were now filled with the Spirit of Truth and of Love. The very communion that binds the Son to the Father now embraces us. Filled with the Spirit, we can now become perfect as the Father is perfect, merciful as the Father is merciful. We can now love God as God had loved us.

• *Have you ever had, because of your faith in Jesus, a life-changing experience, a real transformation, like being "born again?"*

• *Why is the gift of the Holy Spirit so important? Do you have a personal devotion to the Holy Spirit? Should you?*

The same divine favor that willed the Incarnation also willed the means for that redemptive love to reach every human person for which it was intended. The Church then is part of the Mystery of the Incarnation, and so are its ministries. The deacon, in particular, embodies in the communion of the Holy Spirit, the form of the Incarnation, the servanthood of Jesus Christ. The deacon becomes the living sign of the flesh of the incarnate Word, in all its humility and self-emptying, even unto death on the cross. In this, the deacon is also the sign of our forgiveness, of the solidarity through which we have been saved. Where there is need, there is the Christ; and where there is the Christ, there is salvation.

- *How is the Church, born from the side of the crucified Jesus, the "new Eve," the Mother of all the living? Do you ever think of yourselves, as members of the Church, to be the children of a new humanity? What difference might thinking this way make?*

- *What does it mean to you to see the deacon as a sign of the humility and self-emptying of Christ? How do you think Christ would judge a proud and self-serving deacon?*

- *How is the deacon a sign of our forgiveness? How might a servant ministry practically be also a forgiving ministry?*

- *Besides signing the servanthood of Christ, the deacon might rightly be considered the sign of a new humanity? Try to express what this means and what it adds to our understanding of the diaconate.*

Both the Christian married couple and the deacon stand before the one Word of God, the one Lord Jesus Christ. Each in their own way is born of the one call into personhood, and of the perfection of it that is the new life bestowed in Christ. Each has known the burden of human sinfulness and has been shaped by the grace of divine forgiveness. Both are inextricably part of the mystery of creation and redemption, as they sign, each in their own way, the unity between God and man that is the incarnate Word, the Lord Jesus Christ.

> • *In your own words, try to express what both Christian marriage and the diaconate have in common in God's plan for human persons.*

Even though the context of their witness to the perfection of humanity and the form of the redemption is different, it is merely a difference in human situation and of purposefulness in the community of the Church and of the world. Distinct from one another, they remain united in the common ground of their witness to the perfection of love. Both love-become-service as the goal of Christian married life and self-emptying-service as the form of the diaconate in the Church are human expressions of what is in essence the nature of God as we have come to know it through revelation. They cannot be played then one against the other. What fulfills and perfects one will ultimately fulfill and perfect the other.

> • *If what fulfills and perfects Christian marriage also fulfills and perfects the diaconate, what is the advantage in joining the two? What is the benefit of the union and who is it that benefits from it?*

> • *Since you, as a married couple, have joined the diaconate to your marriage through the ordination of the husband, how is the Church the better for it?*

Conclusion

We need now to return to the very human problem with which this essay began. How one man might harmonize and unite in a truly integral manner the responsibilities and obligations of Christian marriage with those of the diaconate is the question that I sought to clarify and, as well as I could, contribute some thoughts toward a resolution. Criticizing the prioritizing of responsibilities, which I consider part of the problem, would prove pointless on my part and frustrating to the reader unless I can show how we might replace the listing of God, wife, family, work, and ministry with a decision making model that is integrative, clear, and practical.

- *How have you as a married couple been making the important decisions that face you in your married and family life?*

- *Has anything is this essay helped you to rethink how you make decisions?*

• *With the added responsibilities of the diaconate, do*
you think that how you have been making decisions
will continue to serve you well?

For all I have said, the concern in the end is practically
that of one individual human being who happens both to
be married and ordained. As human, naturally constrained
by the limits of space and time, he will always be able to
do only so much. His every "yes" cannot but be accompa-
nied by several often regretted noes, said somehow, some-
where, to someone. While there is no escape from such a
limitation, even a finite human being, I daresay, is meant
to live with integrity, fulfilling the responsibilities that genuinely are his. I have come to believe there is only one
way to do this, to avoid compartmentalizing life, playing
off one responsibility against another, and that lies within
the mystery and unity of our personhood.

• *How have you dealt with the noes you have had to*
say of necessity to the people that are part of your
life? As a couple? As individuals?

• *What does "being a person" mean to you?*

Being a person is greater than the sum of our strengths
and the splendor of our achievements. Our personhood
has its origin in a personal God. For all that is different
between God and ourselves, who we are and what we are
capable of ultimately corresponds to the nature of our Creator, to what God is. We worship a tri-personal God whose
essence is love and who has actually loved us into existence. We too are persons, beings created for love, that we
might not only freely and consciously return the gift of
love to its source, but also ourselves participate in the

mystery of loving others into existence and into freedom. And so we need, like all the mystics, to gaze beneath the surface of our humanness and discern there the flow of love that begins in God, moves into us as a gift, and flows from us into the lives of others, returning to God as a living sacrifice of praise.

- *Do you believe that "being a person" is about what we share with God, about what God and we have in common? Talk about that for a while.*

- *Do you agree with the assertion that the heart of our personhood is our capacity for love?*

- *Life is all about love. True or false? Explain your answer and how you understand it to each other.*

It is this movement that makes our story truly awesome. All our bible stories, all true growth moments of our lives, all of them are about persons fulfilling their personhood in the perfecting of their love. The gift of divine love individuates us, bestowing upon us not only our personal uniqueness, but also our integrity as an individual subject, an individual actor and lover. The final perfecting of our love comes in and through our personal union with Jesus Christ, in whom all fullness resides, the exemplary lover, who loved us even unto death upon the cross. Here we have then both the origin and the goal of our temporal pilgrimage, the ultimate meaning of our lives, which is meant to give direction and purpose to every phase of our journey.

• *Share some examples from the Bible of individuals finding fulfillment in the perfecting of their love. Old Testament? New Testament?*

• *Does it make sense to you to say that being loved and being a lover is what makes us the unique individual person that we are? How have you experienced this?*

• *Has your relationship with Jesus made you a better lover? How so?*

A man and a woman marry. Whatever the reasons that they first met, were first attracted to one another, fell in love, and said "Yes" to "Will you marry me?", they embarked on a journey designed from the beginning to perfect their ability to love and, through the grace of Jesus Christ and the power of the Holy Spirit, to witness the perfecting of that love to one another and to their children.

A man is ordained a permanent deacon. Whatever the reasons that he first presented himself, began a program of formation, matured through the hours and demands of preparation, and said "Present" to the calling of his name before the Bishop, he embarked on a journey designed from the beginning to perfect his ability to love and, through the grace of Jesus Christ and the power of the Holy Spirit to witness the perfecting of that love to the Church and to the world.

• *What's the same in both situations?*

• *Granting the differences, do you think that both of these situations can really be lived as one? Take some time together on this one.*

A married man and a deacon are situationally distinct and differently engaged in the liturgy that is life. Yet in the light of the mystery of creation and redemption they both have been structured by the self-communication of God. As persons they share a common origin and purpose, both ordered to the perfecting of love in a limited and sinful humanity by a free and abiding commitment to love-become-service.

Whatever may be the multitude of our responsibilities, as personal subjects we make only one spiritual journey, having only one life to live. A man, joined to a wife in Christian marriage and ordained to the diaconate in apostolic ministry, remains the same individual person, one subject pursuing one ultimate purpose. Although expressed in diverse settings, he makes only one journey through love-become-service to the perfecting of human love in and through Jesus Christ. His increased responsibilities upon a broader field of action and opportunity are not meant to divide his heart. If love-become-service, moving toward perfect love of God, is what he is meant to be about in all that he does, both as a married man and as a deacon, then listening to the promptings of that love and acting upon them is the key to his integrity and the harmony of his life.

- *Do you agree that these two life situations find their unity and harmony in the common origin and purpose they have in God? Have you experienced this already in any way?*

- *A husband who is a deacon is not two people. Right? How important then is it for him to have one reason for doing what he does wherever he does it?*

- *How important is listening as a first step in decision-making? Share some examples from your own life?*

- *What happens when you decide without listening? Share your experiences of this.*

Marriage and the diaconate are not two paths upon which the married and ordained man journeys, choosing one over the other, according to the circumstances. Paths remain separate ways, even if they traverse the same landscape. The traveler still chooses, preferring one over the other, for whatever reasons. While he walks upon the one, he abandons the other. The man who is husband and deacon, pursuing the perfecting of love in the one life that is his, is rather like a musician who blends several distinct sounds of different pitch and quality into a single chord, a sound that is new to the ear and otherwise impossible to evoke. Marriage and the diaconate can be harmoniously united if they are brought together by a willing and personal surrender to love-become-service. Such a person will become incapable of playing off one responsibility against another, forgetting one commitment by becoming absorbed in another. He will bring forth something wonderfully new, for his family and for the Church.

- *How can "a willing and personal surrender to love-become-service" bring together the many elements of your lives the way a musical chord unites the sounds of different notes? Talk about this for a while.*

- *How does this play out the same for both husband and wife?*

- *How does it play out differently?*

• *Does the harmonious union of Christian marriage and the diaconate create something new? What do you think of this idea?*

The key, of course, will always be the authenticity of his listening, both in his marriage and in his ministry, to the promptings of love seeking perfection, and rightly responding. Listening to the Spirit is the beginning of all holiness, whatever the particular situation of our lives. For the married permanent deacon the voice of the Spirit emerges as the urgency of love becoming service across the breadth of his life and within its commitments. He must respond to that voice, but he must also learn how. It is here that he must turn to the concretization of love-become-service in the particular gift that Jesus Christ has given him in the image of the foot-washer. Here he will find inspiration, guidance, and confirmation.

• *Is the "urgency of love becoming service" a legitimate criterion in our decision-making? Share some examples of when the urgency of a true need shaped your decision. As a couple... As an individual...*

• *Do you agree that we all need the example of Jesus to do this well? Why?*

Although he is both husband and deacon he will never make of them something to be grasped at, held for personal esteem, or as leverage over another. He will empty himself of all need for prestige and recognition. Nothing will be beneath him as he identifies with those he loves and serves. His love will find fulfillment in gestures as apparently insignificant as bringing home bread and milk and hotdog rolls, or a catechism lesson repeated to a group of distracted adolescents. He will be patient when misunderstood and persistent in the face of rejection. Pursuing the perfection of love through service under the tutelage of Jesus Christ, he will unite his marriage and his ministry in a seamless glorification of God.

• *Pause for a moment of silence and then read aloud the passage from Philippians 2:1-15.*

• *How are you being called to live this? As a couple? As a husband and deacon? As the wife of a deacon?*

• *Pray together for a while.*

There is another element in the ministry of Jesus that is very important in responding rightly to the promptings of the Spirit in the pursuit of the perfecting of love through service. As I listen to the Gospel narratives of Jesus' being in the midst of people, I am always struck by his ability to find, often in a great crowd, the one person most in need of his love. A child pushed to the back of a crowd... An ostracized woman at a well... A blind man by the side of the road... A tax collector at a customs post... A widow mourning the death of her son... A crucified thief... It was such as these, and many more besides, that Jesus fixed upon in the urgency of their need. While he taught the many, he always reached out toward the one who was different, who was alone, who needed him. And what he could give them, he gave immediately. The narratives of his Sabbath healings give ample testimony to the price he paid by his refusal to defer the gift that was his to give. I believe that this particular behavior in Jesus was central to his illustration of the love-become-service that was his as the incarnate Son

of God, a key element in his revelation of the shape of
the Kingdom of God.

- *How important is it to be able to find the person with
  the greatest need? In a family? In other settings, like a
  classroom, a social gathering, a prayer service...?*

- *Have you ever experienced this? As the one in need?
  As the one being able to help?*

- *How important is it to respond immediately?*

- *Can you explain how all of this is a revelation of the
  Kingdom? Try.*

It must also be noted that the gift that Jesus gave was, in
the end, a gift that he alone was willing to give. As the person most urgently in need emerged from the crowd, Jesus
also emerged from the crowd as the only one hearing the
need and willing to respond. Jesus sees the needy one, and
the needy one sees Jesus. The crowd evaporates, disap-
pearing into the background, as it did in the Temple when
Jesus intervened for the sake of the woman taken in adul-
tery. Many often are present, but only two face each other
as mercy and need intersect. Part of the mystery of perfect
love is the willingness of the incarnate Son of God to
emerge from the crowd and establish a solidarity with a
specific person in the situation of their need. It is Jesus, and
no one else, who calls the child from the back of the
crowd... who asks the Samaritan woman for a drink... who
follows the cry of the blind man... who eats and drinks in
the home of the tax collector... who gives the widow back
her son... who promises paradise to the dying thief... It is
Jesus, and no one else. When he died upon the cross,

we believe that he saw each of us in our need and in our sinfulness, and called us each by name. "He loved us and handed himself over for our sake." So says the Holy Spirit, in the words of the Apostle Paul.

- *What happens when you see a need but are unwilling to stand out of the crowd and do something? Have you ever seen a need and failed to respond? What influenced you to stay hidden in the background? How did you feel about it all?*

- *Were you ever the one in need and were aware that someone knew your need and was unwilling to help? How did you feel about that?*

- *"He loved us and handed himself over for our sake." What is the power of those words? What is the grace for us in them?*

At the heart of the commitment in Christian marriage and in the diaconate is the willingness to emerge from the crowd for the sake of another. The commitment to love emerges from the miasma of self-serving dreams and merely good intentions and becomes actual, as love becomes service in the stuff of the other's need and life. As the apostles reclined and were settling into their cushions, only one person at the table saw that their feet still had the dust of the road upon them and rose to wash them. It was his willingness to embody the perfection of love that ultimately saved us, lifting us from our sinfulness and joining us by his love to the Father. The willingness of the married deacon to emerge from the background and reveal his love through his service to his wife and family, and to his Church, is equally necessary for him to fulfill his identity and mission.

- *Why must a person willingly emerge from the background and reveal love through service to fulfill his or her identity and mission in life? Do you believe that this is true?*

- *What difference does the truth of this statement make to you? As a husband? As a wife? As a deacon ?*

- *Why is this necessary for the permanent married deacon? Are both of you willing to continue to make this happen? How will you do that?*

One human subject, with multiple responsibilities and commitments, pursuing one purpose in the whole of life, willingly doing all for the sake of love becoming service, fixing on the most urgent need and responding with immediacy, such is the married permanent deacon. Inspired both in his marriage and in his ministry by Jesus as he washes his disciples' feet, he should be able to make the day-to-day decisions to do what he alone can do as he sees the real needs of his wife and family, and of his Church. If this is the heart of his spirituality, I truly believe he will never betray, never not see what he must do, never suffer the remorse of a divided heart. He will find his integrity, and live the harmony of a seamless life. One with his wife and with his Church, he will sing a new song unto the Lord.

I am truly grateful to Linda Schmidt, Debbie Rohner, and Teri Lash, whose straightforward and honest remarks raised the issues that led to this essay. A special thank you also to Deacon Bill Urbine, the Assistant Director of our Office of the Permanent Diaconate, who untiringly reviewed every page as it was written and whose pastoral experience generated the reflection questions. Thanks also to Colleen Kleintop, our Administrative assistant, for her day-to-day assistance and to Christopher May, a deacon candidate and publisher at Dufour Editions, who brought this work to print.

Rev. Msgr. Michael J. Chaback, KCHS, STD, PH.B: Director of the Office of the Permanent Diaconate of the Diocese of Allentown and a Knight Commander of the Holy Sepulchre, Rev. Msgr. Michael J. Chaback is a native of Bethlehem, Pennsylvania, where he attended Saints Cyril and Methodius Elementary School, Bethlehem Catholic High School, and Lehigh University as a National Merit Scholar.

He began his preparation for the priesthood at Saint Charles Borromeo Seminary in Philadelphia and was sent in 1964 by Bishop Joseph McShea to complete his studies at the Pontifical Roman Seminary in Rome. He holds a Bachelor's degree in Philosophy and a Doctorate in Sacred theology Magna cum Laude from the Pontifical Lateran University in Rome.

He was ordained a priest in 1970 by Pope Paul VI on the occasion of the Holy Father's own 50 anniversary. On his return to the diocese, Father Chaback was appointed Associate Pastor of Saint Francis of Assisi Parish in Allentown and Secretary of the Diocesan Tribunal. The following year he was appointed as an Associate Professor at Allentown Central Catholic High School.

In 1972 Bishop McShea released him for service outside the diocese and John Cardinal Krol appointed him an Associate Professor at Saint Charles Borromeo Seminary in Philadelphia. During this time he served intermittently as a Lecturer at Mary Immaculate Seminary in Northampton and DeSales University in Center Valley. In recognition of his service to Catholic Education, Pope John Paul II created him an Honorary Prelate of His Holiness in 1991. In 1992, after twenty years of service at the seminary, ultimately as the Chair of the Department of Systematic Theology and Chair of the Institutional Planning Committee, he returned to the Diocese of Allentown to assume the duties of a pastor.

Bishop Thomas Welsh appointed Monsignor Chaback the tenth pastor of his own home parish, Saints Cyril and Methodius in Bethlehem, where he served for the next sixteen years. During that time, he was also appointed by Bishop Edward Cullen to two terms as Vicar Forane for Northampton County and to two terms as a member of the Diocesan Board of Education. In 2008 he was appointed to his present position as Director of the Office of the Permanent Diaconate.

Notes

Notes

Notes